The Chair

The Chair

Lynne Katz

Copyright 2010 Lynne Katz

ISBN 978-0-557-59017-9

Prologue

For our fiftieth wedding anniversary, Henry crafted a timeless declaration of who we were as one. Timeless, because its essence has always existed and would continue to exist beyond us, to be questioned and learned from and thought about and strived for. It was a poetic version of romanticism for the elderly, an outpouring of love for me and hope for us.

That Henry formulated his emotions in a poem was unusual. He wasn't even particularly fond of poetry, but occasionally, some spoken word or phrase caught his attention, and when it did, it was powerful. My wedding anniversary poem, which he titled "The Gift of Aging," deeply moved us, and we often read it to each other.

The Gift of Aging

In rooted depths, a heritage of generations prior and beyond
Advance and thrive with hope for wisdom growing.
Passion loving. Passion learning.
A gift of aging.
Heartbeat rhythms pacing all that's physical until memories are the pieces left, Scattered.
Inspiring those who want to teach, who want to use, who want to know
The gift of aging.
Some consume the moments passing, but I entwine the years and
Waltz through time with partner mine.
Together we accept the gift of aging.

As partners, it was easy to accept aging as a gift. We discussed how aging was something over which we had no choice but acknowledged our choice to accept it with dignity and grace, rather than resentment and disdain. With a partner like Henry, how could I look at aging as something bad? I know he felt the same about me. We were entwined with healthy connections; connections of love and learning and living. Then, all was severed, and I had no one with whom to waltz through time. It was no longer easy to accept aging as a gift, though I keep trying.

CHAPTER 1

"Evelyn, it's time for your pill, honey," spoken by Maddie, those were not especially welcomed words. Had she said, "Evelyn, your limousine awaits," or "Your filet mignon, prepared medium rare, as requested, is ready," or "The book club is about to meet in the main dining hall," I may have perked up, but she didn't say those things and never does.

Maddie is a skilled and affable nurse who performs her duties with professional subtlety, but her voice speaks words that, though kind by definition, resound harshly in my ears. Each "honey" and "dear" is like a fingernail on a chalkboard. You see, the difference in our ages spans sixty-two years of undiscovered territory for Maddie, and yet she speaks to me as if she has already made those discoveries, as if I am the child, and she is the mother.

I'm Evelyn, Evelyn Elswith Covington, born April 21, 1916. At age ninety-four, my home is a 240 square foot room in Country Lane Gardens Nursing Home. I can get myself to the toilet though with some difficulty. I can feed myself, though awkwardly. I can walk, though unsteadily and with considerable pain. My posture is stooped. I see well enough to watch television and read large print books, and when voices project, my hearing is adequate. Bathing and dressing require minimal assistance, and thus, Maddie has arrived to assist me with my morning preparations.

Far back, barely in memory's reach, I recall acquiring the now-fading independence. I remember skipping rope, running at recess, learning to bicycle, and giggling with friends. I reminisce about getting my driver's license and speeding recklessly, primping for college mixers, flirting, drinking, and studying late into the night. There are so many things I did that I hesitate to admit, but there are those I don't mind telling. I kept lots of secrets from my parents. I still remember so many of those times of years past. Each memory enkindles an emotional awakening, none of which involves a nurse named Maddie assisting me in my bathing and dressing. I have an abundance of wrinkles and sags that don't really bother me, but I am stunned by this journey of years. I am very old, but I remember young.

CHAPTER 2

Since I tire easily and am becoming increasingly more sedentary, and because I reside in a place that maintains life rather than nourishes it, I have hours to reflect upon my age and situation. I think of what I would like Maddie to know and understand about me, to respect about me. I don't want to insult her or hurt her feelings, and my thoughts can so easily fall out of my head before I have a chance to speak them. There's no risk just thinking them, and so, both deep within and at the surface, I carry these introspections as a source of ongoing aggravation.

While waiting for Maddie to finish washing her hands, my eyes glance over at the magazine on my nightstand, opened to page seventy-two. Page seventy-two is a full-page ad for a fabulous motorized wheelchair. It has so many conveniences and comforts. It's a wonderfully thought-out design, and I believe anyone requiring this method of getting around would be delighted with the model advertised. The only problem is the $3300 price. Imagine that! Motorized wheelchairs for those in need are their legs, yet they are too costly for the average person. Shameful, that a necessity should be unaffordable.

Maddie comes over and gives me a light shoulder pat and says, "Evelyn, dear, you have a good day. Don't do anything I wouldn't do." I cringe. I smile. I nod. I keep quiet. Again, I eye that chair.

CHAPTER 3

"Mom, what are you doing sitting by that open window? You could get a chill!" My son, Steven, rouses me from a pleasant daydream. I was remembering how I used to look out my kitchen window while doing dishes. A large blue spruce and several lilac bushes adorned the yard. I was smelling the dream.

Steven never arrives with anything other than a scolding. I know it's difficult for him to see me in this place. I know young people feel depressed visiting their relatives in nursing homes. These places don't smell like lilac bushes.

Every time Steven visits, I can hear his frightened thoughts. He thinks his smile protects me, but he wears it to protect *him*. He feels vulnerable, angry, and perhaps even a bit disgusted. The nursing home calls to him, and he tries to ignore its message. I'd like for him to find his way. He could find my room in total darkness, but he feels completely lost here. Steven prefers to hide from the home, from me, even from himself.

Yes, I need a great amount of help, more than I have ever needed in my life. Yes, I live in a place visitors are happy to leave behind once their visit is over. Yes, I am frail and dependent, but I can still think and talk and listen and have opinions and make decisions and feel all the emotions everyone else does. I just wish Steven would either discuss his fears matter-of-factly, or at least hang them on the hook with his jacket and interact with me as one intelligent adult to another. I want to keep being his mother, one who still has things to teach her son. I long to help him sort through this, but he will have to figure it out himself. Perhaps treating me as the intellectually aware adult that I still am is too much at odds with the order of his world and therefore too scary and too painful.

I'm tired. I imagine how relaxing it would be to sit in that $3300 chair.

CHAPTER 4

"Miss Evelyn, it's time for your therapy (Someone is always announcing what time it is or complaining about my open window). Let's just get you outta your nightgown. Come on, now, Miss Evelyn, it's time to rise and shine."

Oh, I haven't yet opened my eyes, but I know who is there. Bernice, cliché of a nurse. Bernice, robotic charmer. Bernice, obsessively tidy. And that tidiness factor is my biggest annoyance with her. Bernice can't stand a mess, and to her, anything not where *she* thinks it should be is a mess. This is supposed to be *my* room, *my* space. Not many people who enter my space respect that. They behave as if they know better than I what my needs are and as if it is their right to act upon their views.

My niece, Myra, is like that, too. When she visits, she checks to make sure my bathroom is clean before giving me the obligatory hug. She will summon the custodial staff if it's not up to her standards, and if she finds something out of place, I am reprimanded.

It bothers Myra that I leave my hairbrush on the edge of the sink. She puts it on the shelf. I tell her that I like and want my brush on the edge of the sink. She tells me that the brush shouldn't be there. I don't rearrange *her* household items when I visit. And I wonder, at exactly what age does one forfeit the right to have her belongings left alone? Everyone searches for a way to make "it" better, and to Myra, a tidy bathroom is "it;" the elixir for "old ageness."

In a couple of minutes, Bernice will notice my "mess" and berate me. She will rearrange my arrangements. She will relocate my stuff to make it comfortable for her.

"Miss Evelyn, how can you live with such clutter? Here, let me neaten things up a touch." She moves things on my shelves and on the windowsill. She aligns each piece of furniture. "There, now, that's better. Doesn't it look better in here? Doesn't that make you feel better?" I'd really like to answer that question, but she isn't expecting an answer. This is about Bernice needing to have my room feel better for *her*.

As Bernice helps me get out of my nightgown, I notice that the magazine on my bedside table, the one with the expensive motorized wheelchair, is nowhere to be seen. Bernice has probably put it in the drawer. I reach to open the drawer, but Bernice pulls my arm back and tells me we have to hurry up because the physical therapist is waiting. As she wheels me out of my room, I glance at the barren nightstand top and make a mental note to "mess it up" as soon as I return to my room.

CHAPTER 5

Cate is coming today. She's a former neighbor, a very engaging and compassionate woman. She visited me when I lived across the street from her, visited me when I sold the house and moved into an apartment, and visits me at Country Lane Gardens. Hard of hearing, herself, she understands my need for volume and clarity. Cate brings the gift of perspicacity with her.

Her favorite expression is, "Ain't life *intersting*!" and to her, I am those words. I am life. I am interesting. When Cate visits, I feel alive, and I feel interesting. I feel like she wants to be here. She doesn't fidget or try to conceal a desperation to escape the confines of this disagreeable reality. Just like everyone else, the halls call to her, close in on her, but she doesn't fight it. She talks about it, along with politics, reality TV, today's youth, and global warming, and we make up nicknames for the staff on my wing. We never, ever mention the weather.

Before Cate leaves, she invariably inquires if there is anything she can do to make me more comfortable in my room. She doesn't tell me what I need to feel more comfortable. If I ask her to take my hairbrush off the bathroom shelf and put it on the edge of the sink, she will.

Prior to Cate's arrival this morning, I placed the magazine that is usually on top of my nightstand inside the drawer. I haven't taken it back out. Maybe I'll look at it tomorrow.

CHAPTER 6

At about 3:00 PM, I was napping in the recliner by the window. I had drifted off to the smell of lilacs, the sight of a spectacular male cardinal perched on the blue spruce, the sound of water flowing out of the kitchen faucet, and the feel of the hot soapy water on my hands. In our household, I did the dish-washing and my husband did the drying. We had enjoyed our mundane chores together.

Henry had been a university professor and I an event planner for the same university. We met while planning a fundraiser for his department. When Henry's father became terminally ill and was moved to a nursing home, Henry and I became interested in, and subsequently involved in, eldercare issues. The university has its own internationally acclaimed gerontology research center dedicated to improving the quality of life for the elderly. Henry and I donated money and time to their community efforts. I have been thinking that I should visit the chief of operations at the Elder Care Research and Development Center. Maybe she will have some ideas about the chair.

CHAPTER 7

On a bitterly cold day in January, in the hospital, after having suffered a heart attack, Henry died. That was eight years ago. A blast of icy cold chills me anew each time I remember leaving Henry in the hospital and walking outside to where Steven waited. Steven had pulled his black Jeep to the entrance to minimize my discomfort from the blustery winds and subzero temperature. It seemed pointless. I would have endured far worse everyday for the rest of my life over the excruciating pain of this loss. I would rather have had the biting wind whisk me away to wherever Henry was.

Steven had rushed out of the car to take my elbow and guide me inside. He had asked me if I was warm enough or if he should turn the heat up. I had been speechless and just shook my head. At that moment in time, there was nothing powerful enough to warm me or undo that which had transformed my body into a wilted blob of sorrow.

I don't like to discuss or think about what happened then or in the following two years. Sad and painful is explanation enough. Two years was the duration after which I could, most days, find a safe place to hold Henry in my heart without fear of reliving the raw, crushing pain of the loss of my beloved partner.

There are still days when my hand involuntarily reaches up and out, wanting to pull Henry back to me. From where, I don't know, but the impelling force transcends anything I've ever felt.

CHAPTER 8

"Evelyn, every time I come in here, you are looking out that window. What do you look at? There's nothing to see but a brick wall out there. And no matter what the weather, you always have that darn window open. Honey, you are going to get sick having that window open all the time."

Maddie is right, and she is wrong. There *is* a brick wall outside my window, but there's so much more to see. To me, it is a canvas that I paint with my memories, and I can only navigate the scene I create if I feel the outside air on my face. I won't get sick from the outside air coming in, but I *will* get sick if I can no longer wear it.

Before Maddie came in, I was walking along the road in my old neighborhood. We had lived in a rural area, and in 1985, the county bought 100 acres adjacent to our property. On that 100 acres had been a charming little white house hidden behind five mature silver maple trees. A family of four lived there for twenty years.

Once the county bought that property, the family moved away, leaving an empty, but still charming, place. Gradually, it fell into disrepair. The county cut down the trees and hired a company to dismantle the house. First, a work crew came to strip the inside and then the outside of all things reusable: doors, light fixtures, windows, wiring, siding, etc. Then, piece by piece, the work crew tore the shell down and left bare ground.

I had watched the home become less and less a mélange of humanness and more and more a bare and uncommunicative structure. As I observed this transformation, it struck me how the once life-full something had turned into a lifeless nothing. Disconnecting the various wires and pipes and floorboards and doorknobs destroyed the ability of the home to offer what it had once lovingly and artfully been capable of providing. And the destruction of the trees seemed so callously disrespectful of their inherent worth. Sometimes, I think I am that house and those trees.

This might be one afternoon that I'm thankful Maddie was here to interrupt my reverie. I need a diversion, a happier thought. Before she left the room, I asked her to hand me the magazine on my nightstand.

CHAPTER 9

My dream chair has a name: The Glissader4000. I show the picture and describe its features to everyone I encounter. Sometimes, during meals, I describe it to those at my table. They ooh and ahh until they hear the price. Then they exclaim, "So expensive! Who can afford that?" And the conversation goes back to somebody's health troubles. I want to talk about the chair. It is remarkable and can provide the user with such comfort, increased maneuverability, and, subsequently, independence.

I think we should write to the company—and perhaps to congress—and solicit help from our doctors to get the price lowered. Why should our needs be so costly? I don't want to talk about diverticulitis.

CHAPTER 10

"Mom, where do you want to go for your birthday?" Steven asks. Steven visits me weekly; his wife, Pam, comes less frequently. Today, they are both here to celebrate my birthday in our traditional way, by taking me to eat any place I choose.

What I'm in the mood for is a long drive, one that follows a river to a mountain pass that winds up and down and around through storybook farms; one that continues for hours and days and years. I want to press my face to the window and be mesmerized by the mystery of all things living. I want to find a patch of hyacinths, run out of the car, and breathe in the scent. I want a picnic by a river.

"Let's go to that new Italian restaurant," I say. Italian is my favorite food.

CHAPTER 11

I try to connect with people to learn who they are from them, rather than read their faces to guess their thoughts or to have to judge them by mere appearance. We have years of practice reading body language, but once the body begins to visibly deteriorate, its language is foreign, and people shy away in an uncomfortable awkwardness. Relationships make the human experience honest, but the art of connecting and the attempt at honesty are more difficult or even completely lost when the usual cues are altered or missing. Beyond many an elder person's vacant look and limited mobility lies a depth of emotion and fighting spirit just waiting for a challenge, any challenge.

My relationship with my daughter-in-law, Pam, is not honest. She's respectful and dutiful, but she fears old and consequently is afraid to connect with me. Over the course of ten years, Pam watched her parents transform from an outwardly vibrant and affectionate couple to depressed and ailing nursing home residents whose bodies failed them well before their minds; whose physical frailties caused them to be out of reach even though they lived their final years in the same room.

Ever since, Pam has worn a protective shield of unnatural charm and elegance. Twice, I tried to talk to her about her pain, but she laughed it off. "Oh, Evelyn, don't worry about me. I'm fine," she said both times. I think Pam's emotional unhealthiness has pushed my son into a similar category, and as a childless couple, they have no youthful inspiration to balance out the emotional armor they share in common.

It's difficult to understand why something so natural, something that is set in motion from the day we are born, causes so much misunderstanding and destructive turmoil. Some parents start saving for college before their children are even born, and yet how do we prepare for living old?

CHAPTER 12

We seem to be a culture that celebrates youth and closets the infirm and disabled. The closer to perfection, the better and more valued. I'm bothered by the thought that old people are too easily dismissed. And the older you "look" or "act," the more quickly you are dismissed. It's like being excused from the dinner table. You are excused as if life is no longer yours to live. This is the kind of thing that occupies my mind and prompts a myriad of questions for which I am always seeking answers.

Of late, I have been wondering who is old and when is old. These questions kept me awake most of last night, and I came to the conclusion that there are three characteristics that define old in oddly powerful ways: speed, memories, and imagination.

Outside the nursing home, people seem to easily glide past me. They stir up the air, and their breezy whoosh barely announces a presence. If they utter a greeting, some of the words land on me while others fall to the ground. I don't have time to gather them up. All who pass seem to dance lightly and quickly by. I am the tortoise. They are the hares. I think that's the reason I rarely go out. It's overwhelming, confusing, and intimidating.

To have the world run by and to have words carelessly thrown at me, while not being able to collect the pieces and absorb them, is exasperating—no time to formulate a reply. I am still capable of understanding and interacting, but I need time. I am slowing down, and the world is speeding up. At least, that's my perception. But young people don't adjust their speeds. They either aren't aware that they should, or they don't know how, or they don't want to—and I *can't* adjust mine. So, we miss each other in passing, or rather, in living.

As for memories, they are heartwarming treasures and depressing reminders. They are proof of what was before and is no longer. I have memories in my drawers, memories on my walls, and memories on my sons' faces. There is no effort in memories. They just are.

And the imagination part of my definition is what I paint on the brick wall outside my window. That's how I create life beyond the nursing home. It is not forward or backward thinking. It is a tool that allows the real here and now to fade completely while a new one enfolds my being with something easy and palatable and just plain nice. I can no longer drive myself to the grocery store or mall. I can't go visit the library or take myself out for lunch, but I can take myself on endless journeys to places that assuage all my senses in ways that will never happen otherwise.

Young people imagine their goals before setting them, and they imagine opportunities by which to attain those goals. They envision new and better and exciting. They imagine a future. They want to get there fast. Old people plan for the future but try not to imagine it. Old people imagine what isn't and can't be. Young people imagine what could be.

CHAPTER 13

When Henry and I met, it was not love at first sight; not even like. It was more of toleration by force. I was in the midst of planning for his department's annual fundraising event. The previous director of fundraising had recently taken a job in the private sector, and I was next in line for promotion, so it was my first year in charge. The opportunity was grand, the headaches even grander, but I loved my job and was very good at it.

Henry was a professor of biology and taught a full load of classes. There were numerous chances for him to advance into more prestigious positions but all involved research, and Henry's love was the students.

The reason we didn't warm up to each other initially was that Henry hated fundraisers. He was required to help plan and attend these events but begrudged them vehemently.

Henry was my assigned "go-to" person, and every time I had to speak with him about the upcoming affair, I felt like an annoying fly he wasn't able to swat away. Finally, after several rude encounters, I asked his secretary why he was such a grump. She took considerable time to praise this "absolute gem" of a professor who was so gentle and kind. She elaborated on his unique style that endeared him to all who had the good fortune to be in his classes. The secretary's gushing tribute intrigued me because it was miles different from my experience. I even wondered if there was some misunderstanding about whom we spoke. So why, I had asked her, was Henry unfriendly and rude to me? I never forgot her answer. "Evelyn, Henry thrives on his students' energy and idealism. It is this that makes sense to him. Fundraising intrudes on his sense of purpose." I could understand this, and it gave me an idea.

I wrote Henry a letter. This is how it went:

Dear Professor Covington,

The annual biology department gala is fast-approaching, and there are several questions for which I need answers. I realize that addressing fundraising issues is the last task you wish to spend your time on, but unfortunately, it is just one of those things that must be done.

Your reputation as a dedicated and skilled professor, endeared to all your students and colleagues, leaves me in awe, and it is an honor to be of service to you and your department. I hope you can find just thirty minutes to sit down with me so we can finalize a few details that will help make this affair a success.

As director of event planning, it is my job to ensure that university events are set up properly so as to bring in as much money as possible. I take pride in my job and believe in what I do because it is with the funds we raise that you can continue to do that in which you so passionately believe.

Sincerely,

Evelyn Elswith

Yes, my letter was an attempt at winning his cooperation but I meant every word. I wanted him to know that I understood. I sealed the letter in an official university envelope and hand-delivered it to Henry's mailbox. I also placed one pink carnation on his secretary's desk. My encounter with her had expanded my concept of understanding who people are inside and the importance of trying to reach some facet of that inner being. It was just one of many valuable lessons in the whole of the human experience.

The next day, I received a call from Professor Covington. He said, "Miss Elswith, I would like very much to meet with you and answer your questions about the biology department fundraiser. Are you free to meet for coffee in the student union tomorrow at 2:00 PM?" I sure was, and after eighteen minutes over coffee, he had answered each question with the friendliest disposition I had ever encountered, and at 4:30, he walked me to my car. I can't recall what kept us talking for the additional two hours and twelve minutes, but we wanted to see each other again the next day and the day after and the day after that. Seven months later, we were married.

Once, as Henry was telling this story to our sons, I interrupted to take over when he got to the part about my letter. Henry looked quizzically at me and said, "Evelyn, it wasn't your letter that drew me to you." A little hurt and a lot surprised, I asked, "Didn't you like my letter, Henry?" and in a very deliberate and loving way, he replied, "Evelyn, I liked you."

CHAPTER 14

Yesterday, I made an appointment with Eric DeVries, the director of Country Lane Gardens. My appointment is at 1:30 this afternoon. He said he could stop by my room, but I said I would prefer to come to his office. This is official business, and I want it to be construed as nothing less.

I paid Maddie 10 dollars to take my only dress home and iron it for me. My appearance must present a woman who has a serious business mission. One of the nursing assistants helped me get into the freshly pressed dress, and I think I look business-appropriate.

I'm going to leave my walker behind and use a cane to get to Eric's office, which means I'll have to plan more time to get there. The director's office is in another wing, and in addition, I will be carrying a folder with all my notes. I'll have to stop and rest frequently.

This has been a big undertaking for which to prepare, but I'm ready. I am going to explain my case for the Gilssader4000 as a necessity item for the elderly. I will lay out my plan to communicate the need for the manufacturer to work with insurance companies to make it more affordable. In the folder is a copy of the magazine ad, survey results from questions I asked some of the residents, research on other motorized wheelchairs, and some common insurance rules regarding assistive devices. Steven begrudgingly helped me compile the data, though he thinks this (or perhaps me) is a bit nutty. I'm ready, but still unsure as to whether or not my blue shoes would look better.

CHAPTER 15

I'm slightly under the weather today. I woke with considerably less energy and a lack of appetite. When Bernice came in this morning, I told her I didn't feel like getting out of bed, so she just quietly did her usual "unmessing." I didn't much care.

While lying in bed, I thought back to my meeting with Eric. He had greeted me cordially and formally. He never looked at my papers. No matter what I said, I couldn't engage him in the topic. His eyes followed every movement in the hall rather than focus on me. After I finished speaking, Eric had said, "Evelyn, I think we have adequate equipment here and without any extra costs to our residents." I left.

As I walked back toward my room I thought of throwing the folder away and stopped by a trashcan. The receptacle looked more than ready to swallow my passion, but my hand was tightly clenched, mostly in anger, and wouldn't release the papers. I thought how my presence in Eric's office, my carefully compiled data, my freshly ironed dress, and my lack of a walker had not spoken to him. The director only viewed me as the medical chart of an old woman in his charge.

CHAPTER 16

If Steven has a concern about me, he calls his brother, Randall, who lives in Seoul, South Korea; then Randall calls me. Steven lives less than four miles from the nursing home but wouldn't be comfortable calling or driving over to voice a concern. It's foolish and cowardly, but I understand, and I am glad the two are in communication about me.

Randall and I have a reserved openness with each other. Unlike Steven, if something needs to be said, Randall can say it, but still, there are endless things I think need to be said that aren't.

Steven is passive, and Randall is demanding. Steven is tense and serious while Randall is laidback and playful. Steven can be withdrawn while Randall is outgoing. The pattern was set way back when, as children, Randall behaved more like a parent than a big brother. Steven still relies on Randall, and Randall still takes charge.

Randall and his wife, Miriam, are both sixty-one years old; he's a retired high school principal, and she's a former CPA. For the last year, they have been teaching English in Seoul. Two of their three children are married; one is settled in New Mexico and the other in Oregon. My third—and most free-spirited—grandchild leads tour groups in exotic places.

Several times a year, I get lovely letters and phone calls from the two stateside grandchildren. The other one calls on my birthday. Randall sends a Mother's Day card and a birthday card and calls once a month and in-between if Steven has something he wants Randall to convey to me, like last night. Steven had told Randall that I'm ridiculously preoccupied with the motorized wheelchair. When Randall voiced his concern, I could only respond by expressing an enduring truism: the two of you will understand when you are my age. Banal? Yes. True? No question. I asked him to please reassure Steven that I'm fine.

CHAPTER 17

As children, when we balked at being outside in heavy rain, my father told us to just walk between the raindrops. Today, as heavy snow hides my brick wall, I try to guide my eyes between the snowflakes so I can create the destination of my daydream. For some reason, the air on my face and neck is bothersome. I feel that if I can successfully navigate through this snow, I won't feel that frigid air on my skin or in my heart.

It hasn't been a good week. Eric had no interest in my presentation about the Glissader4000. Burt in room 296 died. Someone from housecleaning broke my favorite lamp, one that Henry and I picked out together, and no one will admit responsibility. Margaret from room 295 walked into my room, thinking it was hers, and climbed into my bed and went to sleep. I found her when I came out of the bathroom. Then, a malfunction caused the fire alarm to sound during the middle of the night on Tuesday. Oh, and as I gather from last night's phone conversation with Randall, my sons suspect I'm becoming mentally unstable.

I know unpleasant things happen, and being of an easy-going and flexible nature, I can usually cope, but lately, I feel my expectations and my realities are clashing.

The nursing home is my community; the residents are my neighbors, and the staff are my employees, but this is not a situation of choice. I *have* to live in a nursing home. My only choice is to move to another like community. I can't hire and fire my employees. I can't remodel or redecorate. I can't even lock my own door. Numerous disadvantages accompany this loss of choice and control. Most disturbing is that I am unable to create an identity unique to me. Dependence seems to diminish credibility.

My brick wall offers a form of comfort. I need to get there today. I need to walk between the snowflakes and get there. If any were to land on me, I think the weight would hurt.

CHAPTER 18

Cate dropped by today. It wasn't her usual day, but she had a bouquet of red carnations and baby's breath. She's an intuitive friend who seems to know when I need a visit. I told her all about the chair and my meeting with Eric. Her response was, "Well! I think we should find a nickname for that director!" Cate can always make me smile.

We spent twenty-five minutes anointing Eric with mean-spirited titles, but none was the perfect fit. He deserves nothing less, so we decided to keep thinking.

Cate asked to see my folder and studied its contents. She suggested I go ahead and write to the manufacturer and to my medical insurance company.

The flowers she brought look cheery in the vase on the TV.

CHAPTER 19

Broadway plays couldn't offer better entertainment than last night's dream. I was looking out my window when a Glissader4000 drove up. I climbed out of the window and into the chair and started riding.

    I rode for what seemed hours and days and years until I came to a river. I followed the river until I came to a mountain pass that wound up and down and around through storybook farms. I was mesmerized by the mystery of all things living. Then, suddenly, a patch of hyacinths appeared, and the chair stopped in the middle of them. I closed my eyes and inhaled deeply. When my eyes opened, I was at Henry's grave. A yellow and white checked tablecloth was spread across it with a picnic lunch waiting, and Henry was waiting, too. I walked over and sat on the cloth. Henry and I ate and talked as easily as ever before. He reached for my hand. We studied each other's face. "Isn't my chair grand?" I asked him. "Evelyn, you don't need that chair," he said. "But Henry, don't you like it?" Placing his hand on the side of my face, he looked thoughtfully into my eyes and quietly answered, "Evelyn, I like you."

CHAPTER 20

As Cate suggested, I wrote to the chair company and the insurance company. It took me two weeks to compose and write the letters. My hand shakes, my thinking is often muddled, and convincing someone to look up the addresses was not easy. I never showed the letters to anyone other than Cate, because no one else has grasped the significance of my interest.

I got a reply from the chair company after eleven days. The quick response surprised me, and I was excited to open the envelope. They thanked me for my comments and said, "We will certainly pass your concerns on to our sales department." They also said, "We believe our unique Glissader4000 is superior to any other like machine. It is of the highest quality and the most modern technology which is reflected in the cost. Lowering the price would necessitate lowering the quality." The final blow was, "We have included a voucher for $100 to help with your purchase."

Hmm, so now the Glissader4000 will only cost *me* $3200, but for everyone else in the world, still $3300.

CHAPTER 21

Jordan visits me once a month. He's a darling five-year-old boy who accompanies his mom when she visits her grandmother, Maria. Maria is bedridden and can hardly hear, so Jordan quickly tires of sitting in her room. That's how he and I met. He got bored and wandered, wandered right into my room and my heart.

Per my request, Steven keeps me in supply of Hershey's Kisses, which I give to Jordan when he comes. He'll sit on my bed and carefully unwrap each candy, putting the silver paper in one pile and the white lettered paper in another. Jordan takes me on fun excursions to his kindergarten to meet his friends and to his playroom. I've introduced him to Henry, and we go on picnics, and I've shown him where I used to live. Jordan knows about the Glissader4000. He likes to climb in my lap and be the driver on our trips.

Jordan is like Cate. He's *intersting*, and he likes to laugh. He appreciates life, and he wants to talk about it. He appreciates me and wants to talk about me. Jordan does not talk about the weather.

Today, when Jordan and I were reviewing his school field trip to the children's science museum downtown, Eric poked his head in the room, nodded, marked something on his clipboard, and left. Jordan asked, "What did Mr. Brockowee want?"

"What?"

"That man that was just here."

"That was Mr. DeVries."

Jordan giggled and explained, "Me and my mom made up a name for him. We call him Mr. Brockowee."

"Why do you call him that?"

"Because we don't like him, and we don't like that yucky green vegetable either."

It was my turn to giggle as I thought how absolutely perfect that name was and how Cate would certainly agree.

"Ohhh, you mean broccoli." Jordan nodded his head.

Just then, his mom came to say it was time to go home. She waited by the door while her son gathered up the silver candy papers on my bed and stuffed them into his pocket. He waved and started for the door, then stopped and ran back to me. Jordan studied my face. With hands on hips he angled his head left and then right.

"I'm going to call you Miss Celerwee."

"Why is that?"

Jordan dropped his hands, laughed loudly, and ran for the door. When he reached his mom he turned toward me and yelled, "Because I like *that* vegetable."

CHAPTER 22

Dr. Franklin, my internist, gave me a good report today, though she did say I should see the cardiologist. I told Dr. Franklin about the Glissader4000, and she asked why I was even interested in it since I don't need a motorized wheelchair.

"The chair is so costly. Shouldn't it be more affordable?"

She put her hand on my knee and spoke superciliously, "Evelyn, when the time comes, the nursing home will provide for your needs."

CHAPTER 23

When the time comes, the nursing home will provide for your needs. I have been mulling those words over and over in my head. When is *the time?* Will I wake up one day and be transformed from ambulatory to non-ambulatory? Will a motorized wheelchair appear at my bedside? Who will decide it is *the time?* Does "the nursing home will provide for your needs" equate to "the staff, and the staff alone, will decide what my needs are and when I am in need?" And who is more knowledgeable about nursing home needs than a nursing home resident? And why is utilizing that resource not a priority?

I'm getting increasingly irritated by this whole matter, and I believe people are getting irritated by me. In addition to all this exasperating chair business, I've been feeling so tired lately. I think I'll go to bed early tonight.

CHAPTER 24

Daily operations at Country Lane Gardens are what I refer to as part of the *plan of appearances*. The nursing home has to appear to be in compliance with all state and federal regulations. It has to appear to be keeping its residents busy. It has to appear comfortable. It has to appear to be doing what one expects a nursing home to be doing, and it has to appear satisfactory to the visitors. However, through the eyes of this resident, those appearances are one part deception and one part ignorant inadequacies.

Take Monday mornings. Each Monday, before breakfast, a calendar of activities, a menu for that week, and our morning medicines are delivered simultaneously. The menu uses adjectives like creamy and tender to cultivate good will toward the chef. However, the meals are usually dry and poorly seasoned. The activities calendar promotes bingo as big-time, the ice cream social as sensational, and movie night as magnificent.

Marjorie from suite 214 wheeled herself into my room a little while ago and asked me to join her in the recreation area for Creative Creations (i.e. crafts). I declined, and she complained that I rarely participate in activities and that all I ever do is talk about the motorized wheelchair in my magazine. Marjorie is correct, and there is no explanation I care to give her. Everyone I talk to has the same impression. They all think I should participate more. They all think I look out the window too much. They've all heard my speech about the Glissader4000. They all think it's a dumb and wasteful preoccupation. But shouldn't need receive more attention than appearance?

I concede that the staff's matching uniforms, the artistically decorated bulletin boards, and the attempts to alliterate when describing activities are colorful and chipper, but they are sales pitches. The residents working diligently in the recreation room sorting coupons give a semblance of what non-nursing home residents want to, or think they should, see, but in reality, the life-sustaining stimulation is absent, and the depression rate is high. No one even asks us.

Most of us here are a bundle of fragile old bones. Our bodies need babying, but not all our brains do.

CHAPTER 25

The calendar by the sink in my bathroom displays a squiggly blue check mark on each day without a response from the medical insurance company. Four months and nine days after my letter was sent, I finally got a reply. It was disheartening. "The Glissader4000 is not covered under your insurance policy." They also wrote, "Please call if we may be of further assistance."

CHAPTER 26

My new alumni bulletin was delivered today, and it contained a tribute to an eighty-four year old physician who is affectionately known as Dr. Sidney. He has dedicated his life to the field of geriatrics. He still drives to an office at the Elder Care Research and Development Center. His title is Distinguished Scholar.

The description of the doctor struck me. Words like genuine, soft-spoken, integrity, and humility were inviting to me. Without ever having met him, my decision was made. I had to talk with him. I would call and get an appointment with Dr. Sidney. Since my letter-writing campaign and attempts to rally support from various sources were all abysmal failures, what did I have to lose by trying to get an audience with this renowned gerontologist?

I called the center on Tuesday and actually talked directly to Dr. Sidney. Briefly, I explained my mission and told him I wanted to discuss it with him. This soft-spoken man described in the article, one of the utmost integrity and sincerity, resonated as no less across the phone lines. We set an appointment for 10:30 AM Friday. This coming Friday! Immediately, I called Steven to ask for his help with transportation.

Friday, at 9:00 AM, Steven picked me up. Again, I was wearing my one dress. With my folder squeezed tightly in my shaky hand, I grabbed my cane, and at 9:45, Steven and I stood at the lobby elevator in the Elder Care Research and Development Center. I told Steven I wanted to go to the appointment alone. He said he would ride up with me and wait outside Dr. Sidney's office, but I asserted myself with a firm no. He would have to wait for me in the lobby.

Once off the elevator, it was a bone-wearying trek to the elder scholar's office. The surroundings looked familiar. Not much other than paint color and wallpaper had changed since last I'd been in this building.

When I first appeared in Dr. Sidney's office, he stood up and came around to the front of his desk to greet me. I noticed that he was stooped like me and that getting up and out of his chair was not easy for him. Dr. Sidney shook my hand and then guided me to a seat at a small table. He said he was pleased to meet me, and I believed him. He listened to everything I said, and I know he heard my words. He talked to me about related passions of his while I listened to his words, and I was convinced we had made an honest connection. At 10:55, Dr. Sidney said we should end our meeting but schedule another one in a couple weeks. He said I had many valuable thoughts. I believed him again. We both stood up in our limited and clumsy ways, and I told him my son was waiting in the lobby. He said he would escort me to the elevator.

Slowly, not because one of us required the other to adjust his or her pace, but because that was the pace of who we were, we walked down the hallway together. No one spoke, but the silence was comfortable. At the elevator, Dr. Sidney pushed the button for me, and when the doors opened, I crossed the threshold and turned around to face him. He reached out and rested his hand lightly on the side of my face just as Henry had done in my dream, and spoke with a dignified gentleness, "Evelyn, you are not a chair." We looked intently at each other during those few seconds before the elevator doors started to close, and when they did, he withdrew his hand. His final words were a puzzle, yet I felt something vaguely familiar and stirring in them. As the doors shut all the way, a smile lifted my chin, and though Dr. Sidney was not there to hear, I said, "Thank you."

Epilogue by Maddie

I found Miss Evelyn's papers, along with some Hershey's Kisses, in the bottom drawer of her dresser when I was looking for clothes to give the funeral home. Feeling a little guilty, I sneaked the journal into my purse and took it home to read.

That same night, after everyone in my household was in bed, I sat at my kitchen table reading Miss Evelyn's papers. I read slowly because I wanted to understand. My brain was weighted by the thoughts I tried to absorb. My hands felt the importance of what they held.

After reading the final word, and having smiled a bit and cried a bit more, I put the papers back into my purse, and the next day, I returned them to Miss Evelyn's drawer.

The following Thursday after the funeral, I drove home to my empty house and again sat at my kitchen table, this time reflecting upon the memorial service. Each son had given a loving tribute to his mother. When all those who had wanted to speak were done, Randall had gone up to the podium a second time and said, "Mom was an altruistic woman. This past year, she became passionate about making medical necessities affordable for the elderly and made it her mission to have this wheelchair (he pointed to a new Glissader4000 in front of him) become more accessible to those in need. She was not successful, but in her memory, and to honor those efforts, my brother and I are donating this wheelchair to the Country Lane Gardens Nursing Home." Upon hearing this, I realized that they didn't understand. I wondered if they'd even read Miss Evelyn's journal. As Randall had continued on about his mother's chair mission, I wanted to shake my head and plug my ears, but instead merely stared at the hands folded respectfully in my lap.

So, after the funeral, alone in my kitchen, I needed to connect with Miss Evelyn and let her know someone understood. I closed my eyes, willing her to appear. When she did, I whispered, "You have your new chair, Miss Evelyn, but you never really wanted it, did you? It was never even about the chair."